Ricky ZOOM

RICKY'S NEW BADGE

Adapted by Cala Spinner

ISBN 978-1-338-67740-9

10 9 8 7 6 5 4 3 2 1
Printed in the U.S.A.

20 21 22 23 24
40

First printing 2020
www.rickyzoom.com
SCHOLASTIC INC.

It's an exciting day for Ricky and his friends. Today, the Bike Buddies will have a chance to earn solid gold rescue badges!

"You'll have to be extra strong and fast," Maxwell tells them. "And you'll need to work together as a team."

In the emergency training area, Hank and Helen Zoom give the Bike Buddies a pretend rescue job. The final mission will be to rescue Blip from a tree.

Ricky can't wait. He wants the rescue badge more than anything!

"LET'S ZOOM!" he says.

First, the Bike Buddies move a big pile of sandbags to the other side of the yard. Ricky grabs his bags with ease, but his friends are having trouble.

Next, the Bike Buddies need to untangle a fire hose.
Ricky quickly takes the lead.

"Rev on!" he shouts. The other Bike Buddies
struggle to stay upright.

The last task is the pretend rescue. Blip is dangling from a tree. And he's a good actor, too!

"Help!" Blip yells.

While the other Bike Buddies think about what to do, Ricky gets an idea. "I've got it!" he says, and zips around.

Ricky swoops in and uses his grappling hook to pull the trunk of the tree. He frees Blip!

"Whoopee!" cheers Blip.

"We did it!" shouts Ricky. "We're going to get our badges!"

But Hank and Helen aren't impressed.

"For everyone to earn their rescue badges, you have to work as a *team*," Helen explains.

BEEP! Just then, an alarm goes off. There's a *real* emergency going on. Scootio's Scootbops have gone wild in Maxwell's garage—and they're eating everything!

"Don't worry, kids. We'll handle this," Helen says. Then she and Hank race out.

"Aw, why can't we go?" Ricky asks when they've left.

"Well, we're not rescue bikes," DJ replies.

"But we could be," Ricky says. "If we went and helped, they'd see what a great rescue crew we are, and give us all solid gold badges!"

The Bike Buddies head out.

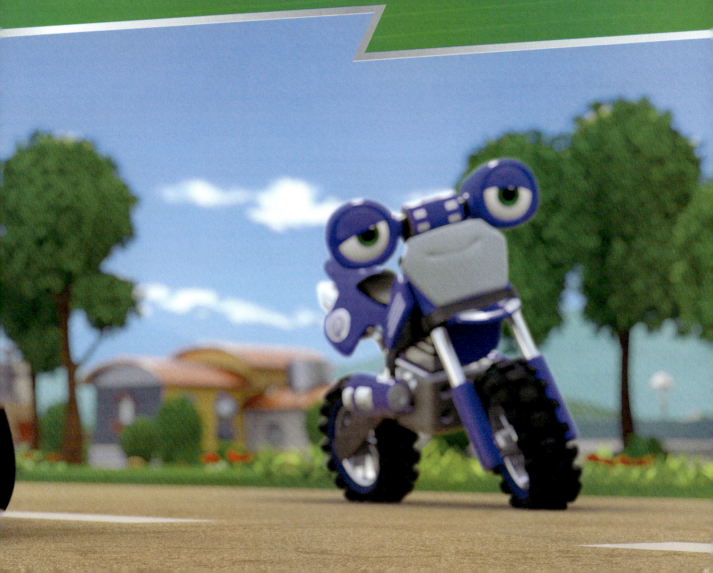

On the way to Maxwell's garage, the Bike Buddies come across Blip, who is being chased by the out-of-control Scootbops.

"Vroom! Ricky to the rescue!" Ricky shouts.

Ricky tries to corral the Scootbops together but he ends up in a bush.

"Ricky, you're a great rescue bike, but sometimes to save the day, you need a team," Scootio tells him.

"You're right," Ricky replies. "And we *are* a great team. I bet we can stop those Scootbops together."

Scootio smiles. "Okay, Rescue Bike. What's the plan?"

"All for one and bikes for all!" says Ricky.

DJ holds up a net and waits while Scootio distracts the Scootbops.

Then Loop confuses the Scootbops by making them chase him instead of Blip.

"NICE WORK!" Ricky calls out to his friends.

Once the Scootbops are all chasing Loop, DJ drops the net right over them.

But the rescue mission isn't over yet—the net doesn't stop the Scootbops!

Ricky is quick. He uses his grappling hook to wrap the Scootbops tighter in the net.

The Bike Buddies did it—together! The Scootbops aren't going anywhere now.

"Zoom-tastic!" Ricky shouts.

Helen and Hank saw the brave rescue. And they have a surprise for the Bike Buddies—their solid gold rescue badges!

"You earned them," Helen says.

"It's all about teamwork," Hank adds.

ALL FOR ONE AND BIKES FOR ALL!

MAXWELL
Ricky ZOOM

BLIP
Ricky ZOOM

SCOOTBOPS
ZOOM

Ricky Zoom © Frog Box/Ent. One UK Ltd. 2020.

Ricky Zoom © Frog Box/Ent. One UK Ltd. 2020.

Ricky Zoom © Frog Box/Ent. One UK Ltd. 2020.

THE BIKE BUDDIES
Ricky ZOOM

MAXWELL'S SERVICE STATION
Ricky ZOOM

SOLID GOLD RESCUE BADGE
Ricky ZOOM

SCOOTBOPS
Ricky ZOOM

The Scootbops are some of Scootio's coolest inventions! These six robot creatures can sometimes make a big mess!

BLIP
Ricky ZOOM

Blip is Loop's big brother! He's always willing to help the Bike Buddies out, but his mail delivery skills need a little work!

MAXWELL
Ricky ZOOM

Maxwell is the town mechanic. Whatever a bike needs, Maxwell will help with a smile and a story about the good ol' days.

SOLID GOLD RESCUE BADGE
Ricky ZOOM

This badge is important— it's about working together as a team! When have you worked together as a team with your friends or family?

MAXWELL'S SERVICE STATION
Ricky ZOOM

Maxwell's garage—or his service station—is where the bikes go to change their tires and get other fixes. Maxwell is always happy to help a bike in need!

THE BIKE BUDDIES
Ricky ZOOM

The Bike Buddies are a group of four friends! They have fun, learn about rescue missions, and take care of each other. This group includes Ricky, Loop, Scootio, and DJ.

Scholastic Inc., 557 Broadway, New York, NY 10012
Made in Jefferson City, USA